THE TOP SECRET DIARIES OF TWIN SISTERS

TWiNNING

AF741176

For Greta – A.M.

Scholastic Australia
An imprint of Scholastic Australia Pty Limited
PO Box 579 Gosford NSW 2250
ABN 11 000 614 577
www.scholastic.com.au

Part of the Scholastic Group
Sydney • Auckland • New York • Toronto • London • Mexico City
New Delhi • Hong Kong • Buenos Aires • Puerto Rico

Published by Scholastic Australia in 2024.
Text copyright © Alexa Moses, 2024.
Illustrations copyright © Sofya Karmazina, 2024.
Designed by Sofya Karmazina.

The moral rights of Alexa Moses have been asserted.
The moral rights of Sofya Karmazina have been asserted.

All rights reserved. No part of this publication may be reproduced or transmitted in any form or by any means, electronic or mechanical, including photocopying, recording, storage in an information retrieval system, or otherwise, without the prior written permission of the publisher, unless specifically permitted under the Australian Copyright Act 1968 as amended.

NATIONAL LIBRARY OF AUSTRALIA
A catalogue record for this book is available from the National Library of Australia

ISBN: 978-1-76129-262-0

Typeset in KG First Time In Forever, Schoolbell Pro, DK Harimau Dua, Pacific Northwest, Esmeralda, Trash Hand, Margarine.

Printed in China by Hang Tai Printing Company Limited.
This product is made of material from well-managed FSC®-certified forests, recycled materials, and other controlled sources.

FSC www.fsc.org MIX Paper | Supporting responsible forestry FSC® C023121

10 9 8 7 6 5 4 3 2   25 26 27 28 / 2

THE TOP SECRET DIARIES OF TWIN SISTERS

TWINNING

by ALEXA MOSES

BFFs (NOT)

Illustrated by SOFYA KARMAZINA

A Scholastic Australia Book

Grace

Wednesday, 3.45 p.m.

My very own diary—I'm so excited! I guess I'd better introduce myself. I'm **Grace Tomic**, I'm 10 years old and I'm in Year 5 at Rocky Point Primary.

The first thing people notice about me is that I'm an **identical twin**. My sister Izzy and I are almost always together and we're closer than BFFs. But even though we look alike, we're not similar **at all!**

Izzy

- Loud and chatty
- Messy (never makes her bed)
- Wears athletic gear
- Likes sports, winning, double-bacon burgers with extra bacon, waking up early, running everywhere
- Thinks homework is optional

Me (Grace)

- Quiet and dreamy (Dad calls me a 'deep thinker')
- Neat (I make my bed every morning)
- Wears fashionable outfits
- Likes reading, art, vegetarian food, sleeping in, doing things thoughtfully
- I'd freak out if I forgot my homework

My sister Izzy and I get stared at wherever we go. On the street, people whisper. At the shops, kids point. Bus drivers look twice when we get on the bus. Someone always says: '**You're twins!**', and Izzy and I try not to giggle. Do they think we haven't noticed? We get asked the same questions over and over, so we have our responses ready.

FIVE THINGS PEOPLE ALWAYS ASK TWINS

1. Are you identical twins?

2. Can you read each other's minds?

(It's actually me, though.)

Izzy and I have to keep our faces straight, which is tricky.

Anyway, the most **brilliant** thing happened today—every kid in Year 5 has to keep a **diary** for the whole year! I couldn't wait to start, so on the way home from school I bought this notebook and three new pens.

Izzy and I share a bedroom, which can be tough because I hate Izzy's mess. So right now, I'm curled up in the cosy egg chair on our balcony writing this, with our cat, **Zeus**, snoring next to me. Our big sister, **Elodie**, is in her room, practicing scales on her trumpet. Everyone else is out.

Anyway, I want Izzy and Dad and Mum to get home because of the second exciting thing that's happening this week.

HARMONY DAY is coming up on Friday and this year, Rocky Point Primary is doing tons of activities! There will be origami lessons, a food stall with treats from different countries and an indigenous basket-weaving workshop.

But the most excellent part is that our principal announced a **competition** for Years 5 and 6. The student who does the best presentation about a different country or culture wins **$100!** That would take months to save up.

If I win the voucher, I'm going to buy the **artist's oil-paint set** in the window of Rocky Art Supplies. The colours are gorgeous, and they have pretty names like Cinnabar, Rose Madder and Viridian Green. If I mixed Ultramarine with Aqua, I'd capture the colour of the sea. **Grazilian Blue**, that's what I'd call my new colour.

If I got that set, I'd hike up to Rocky Point to paint the sea in Grazilian Blue. Joggers and dog-walkers would stop to watch me paint in gorgeous, thick strokes.

Anyway, I have to win first. I've chosen France for my speech because it's **SOOOO ROMANTIC** and has the best art, food and fashion in the world. One day I want to go there, and the first thing I'll do is have a picnic by the **Eiffel Tower**. Mum told me it's a famous tall tower that everyone goes to when they visit Paris!

Très dreamy! '*Très*' means 'very' in French. I know this because I'm learning French on the language app on Dad's old phone.

For my presentation, I'm going to act like a tour guide taking the audience around France. This is how my talk begins: '**Bonjour!** Welcome to France, the country of art, beauty and fashion.'

Izzy and I have planned our presentations **IN SECRET** and we'll reveal them tonight in front of the whole family, which is why I want everyone to come home.

I'm quietly confident my talk will be **the best**. Yes, Izzy's better at performing than me, but she leaves her talks until the last minute, then makes up a **rap**. I'd never say anything to her, but her raps aren't great.

Izzy went to the school library this afternoon to work on her talk. I'd waited with our friend **Otti** for her to get picked up after school.

'You know how I forgot to do the "World Around Us" project?' Otti had said. She was practicing dance steps, using the school fence as a barre. 'Well, Mr Rafael said I have to "**contribute something meaningful**" to the Harmony Day activities to make up for it. What should I do?'

Otti can't remember a single continent on the map except our own. It's not her fault. It's just the way her brain works.

'How about the Harmony Day competition?' I'd suggested, as Otti did little circles with her feet. 'You could do a talk on India, or Japan, or Germany or even America.'

Otti's mum is from India, her dad's parents are German and Japanese, and Otti was born in America.

She'd shaken her head—Otti **hates** speaking in public.

'Then why not **bake** something for the food stall?' I'd said. 'You've got heaps of cultures to choose from.'

She'd brightened.

'That's a great idea, thanks, Grace!' Otti had said, as her mum pulled up in their car. She'd waved as she tossed her dance bag into the boot.

Oh, I wish everyone would hurry up and get home! I miss Izzy when she isn't around.

Mum likes to tell people the story of how Izzy and I **didn't talk** for ages when we were babies. She and Dad even took us to the doctor. The doctor had watched us, then laughed. We *were* talking, she'd said, just not in English. We were speaking a **TWIN LANGUAGE** only we understood and that would disappear as we got older.

The TOMIC-TWIN DICTIONARY

Ziz	Izzy
Gee	Grace
Mee noo	I understand
Gooloo	Good luck
Waah	Dog
Ook	Cat
Mee noo noo ga lem	I want to eat
Baebae	Bedtime
Eepug	Goodnight, sleep tight
Eena-nah	That's disgusting!
Mee ji	I'm sorry
Zizangee	The two of us together

The doctor was right. By the time we reached school, we weren't ZIZ and GEE anymore—we were plain old Izzy and Grace. We don't talk in our special language anymore, except at night. When we're almost asleep, we always say **goodnight** in twin. It's the cosiest thing ever!

Izzy

~~Tuesday~~
Wednesday night

I can't believe school's making us keep a **DUMB DIARY!** Our teacher, Mr Rafael, was so pleased about this **dopey** assignment. He said it would make certain students more thoughtful and mature . . . then looked straight at me!

(If you are reading this, Mr Rafael, please **don't** read any more. You said you'd only check we were writing our required number of pages, not read them. If you promise to stop reading, I promise to catch up on my Maths homework ~~tomorrow~~ ~~next week~~—OK, maybe never.)

(And yes, those are grease stains from the popcorn I'm eating, but, Mr Rafael, why are you still reading this?)

(AND IF YOU ARE ELODIE-SMELODIE TOMIC, PUT THIS DOWN IMMEDIATELY BECAUSE YOU ARE A DIRTY MEGA-SNOOP!!!)

At lunch, Grace got dreamy-eyed about keeping a diary and this afternoon, she even bought a book with a purple cover especially for it. **No way** am I wasting my pocket money on school! Grace thinks writing a diary will be like talking to the most caring friend ever. Um, excuse me, how can 120 blank pages be like a friend? A book can't even answer back!

But since this evening's been a **DISASTER**, I'll give anything a try. That includes hiding in the garage under Dad's old desk and scribbling in the back of my Maths book.

Now, about my terrible evening. After school, I went to the library to check a few facts for my Harmony Day presentation. Our principal, Crome Dome, announced a competition last week and there's a prize of a **$100 VOUCHER** that can be used at any shop in the local area!

I'm going to use the prize money to buy these awesome soccer boots, the **Mercury Quicksilvers**. They're silver and blue, with grippy studs that make you **ZOOM** across the pitch. I'll run so fast and score so many goals that the whole world will hear about me! The national girl's soccer team will beg me to be their **star striker!**

I figure Clover Williams, my **ARCH-ENEMY**, is my main competition in the Harmony Day presentation. Don't get me wrong, Grace works super hard, but she's too quiet to make a real **splash**.

Of course, the first person I ran into at the library this afternoon was Clover, sucking on a red lollipop. I can't even write about Clover Williams without **grinding my teeth**.

Clover Williams, 10

- ★ Mean streak as thick as a skunk's
- ★ First one in our year with a mobile phone
- ★ Sucks up to grown-ups
- ★ Has to be the best at EVERYTHING!

My gaze had gone straight to Clover's schoolbag. There, beside the zipper, hung **MY SQUISHY HAMBURGER KEYRING!**

I am still soooo angry about the **Great Squishy Hamburger Keyring Incident**. It happened like this: Last year, Baka, which is what we call our grandmother, went to Europe and brought us back presents. I'd gotten a squishy hamburger keyring, because I love hamburgers. I'd hung the keyring on my schoolbag and every time I'd looked at it, I'd felt happy. Back then, Clover Williams and I had been friends—I'd thought she was **super fun** to hang out with—even though it was awkward because Grace and Clover didn't get along. But then, on the last day of term, my squishy hamburger keyring had disappeared off my bag! I was **SUPER UPSET!** Our teacher had made the whole class search for it, and Clover had looked hardest of all. She'd acted soooo kind, walking with me to retrace my steps from the moment I'd walked in the school gate that day. But we hadn't found it. My keyring was **GONE**.

Our family had gone away for the holidays, so I hadn't seen Clover for a few weeks. Then, on the first day back at school, Clover had waltzed into the playground . . . with **my squishy hamburger keying** swinging from her backpack! Clover had sworn it wasn't mine. She'd said her mother had bought it in Koreatown on the weekend.

AS IF! After that, our friendship was **over**. I'd complained to our teacher, but she'd said it was wrong of me to accuse Clover of stealing without proof. There might be hundreds of squishy hamburger keyrings in the city, she'd said.

But I KNEW that was *my* keyring. I also knew Clover Williams was a **DIRTY, THIEVING RAT** and I couldn't believe we had ever been friends!

This afternoon, I stared at **my** keyring until Clover noticed me. She took the lollipop out of her mouth and smiled.

'Oh, hi, Izzy,' she said. 'Come to work on your presentation? If you win the prize, maybe you can afford **your very own** squishy hamburger keyring.'

I wanted to tear that lollipop off her and chuck it across the library. Then I remembered what Grace says: if **I** lose my temper, **I** look silly and Clover wins. So I stalked off in the other direction, past Ms Phillips, the librarian, who was sitting at her desk.

Ms Phillips had barely glanced up from the book she was covering, and said, 'Hi, Grace.'

Even though Grace and I have different styles, people who aren't paying attention sometimes **MIX US UP**.

'Hi, Ms Phillips,' I said.

Ms Phillips looked at me properly.

'Izzy? Lovely to see you in the library,' she'd said in shock, as if she'd seen me score a **BACKFLIP PENALTY** in soccer. (A backflip penalty is an amazing move. Everyone will stare in shock when I pull one off—which I haven't done yet, but I will. Soon.)

'Thanks,' I'd said, a little upset. I don't go to the library much—well, ever—but does Ms Phillips think I never read? Cause I do! (~~Sometimes!~~ OK, hardly ever.)

After we'd sorted out who I was, I'd dragged out some history books and taken them into the infant's storytime area, away from Clover. I'd gone to the library to find details to add to my talk. I don't usually bother doing presentations until the night before, but this was different. This was a **competition** and no-one enters a competition to come in **second place**. I'd do anything, even read history books, to get those soccer boots.

And tonight I was going to wow my family with my **BEST PRESENTATION EVER!** Grace and I had kept our Harmony Day presentations **super-secret**, to make tonight especially fun and revealing.

By the time I'd gotten home, Dad was tossing noodles in the wok for dinner. Mum was getting changed upstairs, and my evil big sister, **Smelodie**, was at the dinner table scowling at her book.

As I dumped my bag, **THE EVIL ONE** looked up from her book.

'Oh, hello, Isabel,' she said in a snooty voice, like she was a grown-up. 'Why are you so late?'

I glared at Smelodie. She was only calling me **THAT NAME** to torture me.

See, everyone in my family knows how I feel about **THAT NAME**: the one on my birth certificate. 'Isabel' is a pink, frilly name. Since I'm not a pink, frilly person, I call myself **Izzy T**, which will be my name when I'm a famous **hip-hop artist**.

Smelodie says Izzy T sounds like a brand of baby clothing. Did I mention that Smelodie is **EXTREMELY ANNOYING?**

Izzy's VILLAIN SCALE

(BWA-HAA-HAAA!)

Clover Williams – Perfect **10**

Smelodie Tomic – **9.5**

Clem Chau, Clover's best friend – **9**

Mr Rafael – **8.5** ← (SORRY, NOT SORRY)

Mrs Allsop, nasty school secretary – **8**

Crome Dome, drippy principal – **7**

Harper De Sousa, Clover's second-best friend – **6**

I was about to snap back when I remembered I'd taken Smelodie's skateboard on the weekend without asking. Then, as I was doing a **wicked grind**, one of the dumb wheels had cracked itself.

So I smiled at Smelodie instead, and said in a nice voice, 'I was in the library working on my presentation.'

Smelodie's eyebrows **shot up**. First, I **NEVER** went to the library. Second, I was **NEVER** polite to my big sister.

'What are you hiding?' she asked, suspiciously.

Even Grace, who was on the rug patting Zeus, looked surprised. She opened her eyes the **tiniest bit wider** at me. I shot Grace a return glance.

Some people believe twins can **READ EACH OTHER'S MINDS**, but that's rubbish. What we *can* do is talk to each other **without words**. Grace and I had just had a conversation with our faces. Grace had asked me, *What's going on?*—I hadn't told her about Smelodie's skateboard—and I'd answered, *Tell you later. Just act normal in front of the Evil One.* So Grace kept patting Zeus, who purred like a boiling kettle.

After we'd eaten and done the dishes at **TOP SPEED**, Grace and I hurried out to the living room.

'Presentation time!' Grace sang out.

'You promised, guys,' I added.

Smelodie started to moan about homework, but Mum shot her a warning look. **GO, MUM!**

'Let's get our costumes on,' Grace said. She was pink with excitement.

'I'll get changed in the bathroom,' I said.

Grace and I arrived in the living room at the same time to find Mum, Dad and Smelodie **snuggled** on our saggy sofa.

'Why don't you go first, Iz?' Mum said.

'Is that OK?' I asked Grace.

'Sure,' she said, and plonked down on the sofa beside Mum. Zeus head-butted Grace's knee, and she heaved her onto her lap.

I straightened my beanie, pulled my palm cards from my pocket and began.

'Today is a truly **magnifique** day, because we, the French peasants, are taking back our country!'

More than two hundred years ago, the French peasants rose up and took control of France from their rich king. **THE FRENCH REVOLUTION** was bloody, and gruesome and pretty interesting, at least for history, which is mostly mouldy, old and **boring**.

'Today is the first day of the new Republic! **Vive la revolution! Vive la France!**'

When I glanced up to see how it was going, I got a **shock**. Grace looked as if she'd swallowed a bee!

'What?' I said to her.

She sprang off the sofa, forgetting the cat. With an angry yowl, Zeus tumbled off her lap onto the rug.

She was **REALLY UPSET**, which was weird and awful since Grace hardly ever gets upset, especially not with me. In fact, she's usually my biggest fan.

'You can't do France! I'm doing France!' Grace said.

She grabbed a **beret** from the sofa and jammed it on her head.

'See?! I'm a tour guide showing everyone the famous sights of France, like the Eiffel Tower and the Louvre museum!'

That's when I realised what her outfit was about!

'OK, but why do *you* get to do France?' I said.

'Because I've got a chance of winning!' Grace shot back.

Whoa, talk about **RUDE!**

Mum always talks about Dad and the '**Tomic Pride**'. See, Dad's an easy-going person, except when someone says he can't do something. Then he gets stubborn and refuses to give up. Baka told us that when he was our age, Dad rode the rollercoaster at the theme park **twenty-three times** in a row, being sick the whole way. All because his brother said he couldn't do it.

I felt that

TOMIC PRIDE

kick in.

'How do you know I can't win?' I said hotly. 'I started working on my talk right after Crome Dome announced the competition, and it's **really good**.'

'Please don't call your principal that,' Mum said. 'He can't help being bald.'

Grace and I barely heard her.

Smelodie rolled her eyes. 'France is hardly **original**, you guys,' she said, picking up her book and heading towards her bedroom. 'At least ten other kids will be doing it.'

Mum got up from the sofa and put one hand on my shoulder and the other on Grace's.

'Can't you **both** do France?' she asked in a reasonable, let's-all-get-along voice.

'**NO!**' we both said and ripped our shoulders away.

'Why not?' Mum asked.

We glared at her.

'The teachers **already** hate choosing between us—' Grace said.

'—so if we do the same country, we've got **ZERO** chance of winning!' I finished.

Mum sighed, then walked into the kitchen to put the kettle on.

'Mum, tell her I get France!' I begged, following her. 'I've spent sooooo many hours on my presentation.'

'I've spent more hours!' Grace yelled. 'Many more hours! And why am I the one who always has to **give up** what I want for Izzy?'

Everyone's eyes **bulged**—Grace hardly ever yelled. Mum and Dad shared a look.

'Stop yelling,' Mum said sternly, taking two mugs from the cupboard. 'Girls, surely one of you can do another country?'

'Your mother's right,' Dad said. 'I'm sure you can figure this out if you have a rational discussion.'

Grace stomped out of the living room and down the corridor. Everyone jumped as our bedroom door **SLAMMED**.

I flopped onto the couch.

'Give her a bit of time, Iz,' Dad said, rubbing my back. 'You can talk it over when she's calm.'

Still, he didn't seem sure. Like I said, Grace **hardly ever** gets mad. Perhaps that's why everyone gets a teensy bit nervous when she does. Even Zeus was padding in circles and giving worried **meows**.

When Mum sat back down, I put my head on her shoulder and watched the news with her and Dad. But Grace didn't come back out.

A bad feeling settled over me, like a heavy blanket. I **HATE** fighting with Grace!

So I grabbed some popcorn and came out here to try writing in this **STUPID DIARY**. And maybe Mum's right. Maybe we could both do France.

'How are you feeling?' Mum asked, poking her head into the garage.

'**Not great**,' I said.

'Well, don't let the Tomic Pride decide for you,' Mum said. 'Even when you and Grace compete, you don't have to be enemies—you can still support each other. Remember, you're **stronger together**.'

Maybe Mum has a point.

Grace

Wednesday, 8.56 p.m.

I am **très dérangé!** According to the French language app, that's how you say, '**I am beyond annoyed!**'

I've snuck out of bed and I'm sitting on the edge of the bathtub writing this. After Izzy and I had our fight, something even worse happened. I was at my desk with my doona wrapped around my shoulders, staring at the sunset and counting the times that Izzy had got her way instead of me. I was up to **fourteen** when Dad walked in and ruffled my hair.

'Hi, Gee,' Dad said. He set something on the desk in front of me.

I picked it up. It was an **old photo** that showed two girls dancing in funny costumes.

'Who are they?' I asked.

Dad leant over and switched on my desk lamp. The photo was flooded with light, and I got a jolt. The two girls looked **exactly** the same.

'That's Baka and your Great-Aunt Vesna when they were your age.'

Yes, one of them—who knew which?—was a girl version of my grandmother dancing with a **copy** of herself.

My grandmother, Baka, is Dad's mum. She comes from a country in Europe called **Bosnia and Herzegovina**. Like me and Izzy, Baka has an **identical twin**, Great-Aunt Vesna, who I'd only seen in photos. As older ladies, Baka and her sister don't look so identical. Great-Aunt Vesna looks like someone who can change the tyre on an eighteen-wheeler truck, while Baka loves chunky, gold earrings and high heels—she isn't the tyre-changing type.

'They remind me of you and Izzy in that photo,' Dad said. He touched my shoulder. 'Honey, Baka and Vesna were separated fifty years ago and they still talk every day. They're **closer** to each other than anyone else in the world.' Dad set the photo in the middle of my diary. 'Being a twin is a **RARE AND SPECIAL THING**,' he said. 'Surely your sister's more important than a presentation topic?'

I prickled with irritation. All my life I've heard, 'Grace is such a **GOOD GIRL**,' from my parents, from my teachers, from everyone. Usually I like it, but there's a bad side to it. Dad had come to *me* instead of Izzy, because I was the good twin who'd **give in!**

I folded my arms. 'Remember when we moved into this house and Izzy and I had to choose where we'd put our beds?' I asked. 'Remember last year for our birthday when Izzy wanted a laser-tag party and I wanted an art party? Remember last Friday when you asked what takeaway we wanted? And I can give you **eleven** more examples! Which Tomic twin always **gets their way?**'

Dad sighed. He knew the answer was Izzy.

'I'm not saying you should give up France,' he said. 'Just that fighting doesn't help.'

I tugged the doona tighter around my shoulders. 'If Izzy gives up France, we won't be fighting anymore,' I said with **dignity**, and snapped my diary shut.

Dad took the hint and left me alone.

I was **très dérangé** as I brushed my teeth. I was **très dérangé** as I put on my pyjamas. The longer I thought about it, the more **très dérangé** I became!

When Izzy came in and got ready for bed, I pretended to be asleep, but I knew she knew I was awake. Her bed squeaked. Her covers rustled. There was no whispering or giggling. Instead, there was **SILENCE**. It was a tense silence with a question in it. Would Izzy say our goodnight?

The silence stretched on.

Finally, '**Eepug, Gee**,' came out of the darkness.

For a second I wavered. Then my anger rushed back like a wave on the beach. I knew Izzy was only saying goodnight because she thought that if she was nice, I'd give in and she'd get to do France!

We're too old for that **babyish** goodnight, anyway.

So, without a word, I grabbed my doona and rolled over to face the wall.

Unless Izzy steps aside, it won't be Harmony Day—it will be **UNHARMONY DAY!**

Izzy

Still
Wednesday night,
in bed

Grace didn't say our goodnight!!! *And* she's snuck out to the bathroom and she's been in there for **AGES!!**

What was I **thinking?!** Mum doesn't have a point! What she said doesn't even make sense. As competitors, Grace and I are clearly **ENEMIES!** I reckon Mum was just trying to get me to give up France. **Sneaky!**

Truth is, there's $100 at stake and only **ONE** of us can win. Since Grace loves schoolwork, it's easier for her to switch countries than me. The more I think about it, the colder and harder I get, like a Berry Blast, my favourite iceblock.

Those Mercury Quicksilver boots **WILL BE MINE!**

Grace

Thursday, 11.34 a.m.

Mr Rafael has given us time for our diaries, so I'm writing this **in class**. It's quiet except for the scratching of pens and a few sighs and coughs.

When I went to the playground at recess, I found Sienna sitting cross-legged under the **Friendship Tree**, paging through a fat book. The gold letters on the cover read, *A Complete Scottish History*.

Sienna Burns, 10

- Has a zillion school representative roles
- Loves to study
- Plays the flute
- Wants to be Prime Minister

The Friendship Tree is tall and shady, with a thick trunk that's comfy to lean against and pale green-yellow leaves that whisper as if they're talking to each other in tree language. Usually, a feeling of **PEACE** washes over me as soon as I step under it.

But today, instead of sitting with us, Izzy stalked right past the Friendship Tree and I didn't feel peaceful **at all!** She fished a soccer ball from a tub and stood twenty metres away, bouncing the ball on her toes and shooting **sneaky** glances at us.

Sienna narrowed her eyes. She took in Izzy, then fixed on me. When she sensed anything **unfair** or out-of-place, Sienna was like a sniffer dog who'd smelt a sausage.

'Why isn't Izzy sitting with us?' she asked.

Quickly, I explained.

'Can't you both do France?' Sienna asked.

'If either of us want to win, we need to **STAND OUT**,' I said, folding my arms. 'Identical twins doing the same country is *not* standing out.'

Then Otti bounced over carrying a lunch box.

'Hi, guys,' she said, settling herself gracefully between the tree's roots.

I was about to say hello, when a football smacked into the branches above Sienna's head and dropped beside her. Leaves floated down around us.

'**Be careful!**' Sienna yelled at the boy who jogged over.

'Sorry,' he said sheepishly, scooping up the ball.

'Izzy usually **blocks** those,' Otti said, as he ran off. 'Wait, why is Izzy over there?'

I started to explain again, but then Izzy called out from across the playground, **cutting me off**.

'What?' Otti yelled.

Izzy tried again.

Finally, Otti leapt up and ran around the handball courts to talk to Izzy.

Sighing, I opened my lunch box and plucked a few of the grapes I'd packed for morning tea.

'Izzy said she thought of France **first** and she won't sit with Grace until Grace **gives up** France,' Otti reported on her return. She sat back down in the grass, took off her shoes and pointed and flexed her toes.

Sienna looked at me.

'Izzy can sit where she likes,' I said coolly. 'I'm **not** giving up France. *I* thought of it first.'

Sienna and Otti shared a **worried** glance.

'Can't you both do France?' Otti asked.

'No!' I said, starting to feel **très dérangé** again. Why does everyone keep asking that?

Just then, Otti remembered her lunch box.

'Oh, **look** what I made!' she said, popping open the lid.

'I took your advice yesterday, Grace, and baked **MULTICULTURAL GINGERBREAD COOKIES** for the Harmony Day food stall. Try one!'

'Thanks, Otti,' Sienna said, taking one.

'Multicultural gingerbread is so cute,' I said, selecting another.

'I wish Mr Rafael always let us bake for world studies,' Otti said, beaming. 'It's much more **fun** than memorising maps.'

Sienna and I bit into our cookies and chewed. After a moment, Sienna's face **changed**. She jumped up and hurried over to the hedges by the fence.

'What?' Otti said.

In a second, I understood why Sienna had run.

A **bitter taste** filled my mouth, ending with a **spicy kick** that made me cough. I stumbled over to the hedge to spit out my mouthful.

'What did you put in those, Otti?' I asked, when Sienna and I had sat back down. The horrible taste still coated my tongue and **burned** my throat.

'Rocket fuel?' Sienna added. 'Because my mouth's **ON FIRE!**'

Otti pouted. 'I got inspired by my heritage, like you said, Grace. I used a normal gingerbread recipe and added garam masala and coriander for India, togarashi for Japan and ground cloves for Germany.'

'How much of those spices did you add?' I asked.

'**All** of what was in the little jars,' Otti said. 'Mum uses heaps when she makes curry paste.'

Sienna spluttered.

'Um, I think it's **different** for cookies,' I said.

'Maybe you're just not used to spicy food,' Otti said, lifting her chin.

'Honestly, Otti, you can't sell those. You'll **poison** the entire student body,' Sienna said. 'Hang on, I think Izzy wants something.'

We looked across the playground. Izzy was waving madly at us.

'I'll go,' Otti said, her face brightening. 'Izzy might like my gingerbread. *She* eats **spicy** food.'

'I don't think—' Sienna started, but Otti had slipped on her shoes and darted off.

I peered through my fingers as Otti offered Izzy the box, and Izzy took a cookie.

'Oh dear,' Sienna said.

As she chewed, Izzy's face changed. She **spat** in the dirt, then gestured at Otti, confused.

Otti trudged back and tossed her lunch box under the tree.

'Did you taste them yourself, Otti?' Sienna asked.

'Err . . . no,' Otti said. 'I thought it'd be fun for you guys to try them first, like judges on a BAKING SHOW.'

'Go on, then,' Sienna said, offering her the lunch box.

Otti **nibbled** a cookie. Her face changed and she ran to the hedge to spit it out.

'OK, multicultural gingerbread is gross,' she admitted, mournful as a sad puppy. 'Total baking **fail**.' She collapsed gracefully in the grass.

'Sorry, Otti,' I said.

'I guess I can try another recipe tonight,' she said, sighing. 'Oh, and Izzy says it's not fair we're sitting with Grace instead of her, Sienna. She thinks she should get **EQUAL TIME**.'

'That's a good point,' Sienna said. She checked her watch. 'How about we each sit with a different twin for the rest of recess, then switch halfway? There's **seven minutes** left, so we can swap places at three and a half minutes.'

Like I said, Sienna hates **unfairness**.

'OK,' Otti said. 'I'll take Izzy first.'

Sienna pressed a button on her watch, and Otti set off across the playground for the third time.

'So, are you entering the Harmony Day competition?' I asked Sienna.

Sienna patted the book on her lap. 'Yep, I'm doing a talk on the **complete history of Scotland**, starting three thousand years ago,' she said proudly. Her grandparents were Scottish.

I blinked. Three thousand years seemed an awful lot to cover.

'How will you fit all that history into three minutes?' I asked.

'I'll speak really fast,' Sienna said, with a crisp nod. 'It's all important.' Then she snapped her book shut and fixed me with a bug-eyed glare. 'I know what you're doing, Grace Tomic,' she said. 'You're trying to **distract** me so I don't think about your fight with Izzy. How long are you guys going to keep this up?'

I folded my arms.

'Until Izzy picks another country,' I said. 'Let's be real—my talk's going to be better than hers. Remember her **ANTARCTICA RAP** last year?'

'She shouldn't have **cartwheeled**.' Sienna grimaced. 'That microphone stand hit Mr Rafael really hard on the head.'

'Actually, I was remembering Mr Crome's face when Izzy kept calling him "man",' I said.

We both winced.

'My point is she'll **spoil** my chance of winning if she does France, too,' I said.

Sienna took off her glasses and polished them on her shirt.

'Still, it's not fair to judge this talk by her Antarctica one,' she said. 'This talk might be good. How about Otti and I decide? We can watch your presentations at lunchtime and choose the twin that's **most likely to win**. The winner gets **FRANCE**.'

HIP HOP
Izzy
Thursday lunch,
by the toilet block

I'm soooooo excited! Sienna and Otti are going to have their minds **BLOWN** by my talk!

When the lunch bell went, I ran straight to the Friendship Tree where my friends were waiting. Sienna had a **stopwatch** from the sports cupboard.

'Grace can go first,' I said. Being last means I'll stick in their minds.

'OK, we'll wave at you in five minutes, when she's done,' Sienna said.

So now I'm sitting by the toilet block, **waiting**. The bricks are warm on my back. Better check my watch. Two minutes and twenty seconds have passed.

Grace must have said something funny, because Otti and Sienna are laughing under the Friendship Tree. And when I say 'laughing', I mean, they're **HOWLING!**

I feel sick, like I've eaten a bite of Dad's cabbage rolls (**yuck**) and found mushrooms in them (**yuck** times one million!).

They must like Grace's talk! They must like it a **LOT!**

I'm trying to eat my sandwich now, but it tastes like **cardboard**. Why hasn't Sienna waved to say it's my turn? She must be too busy watching Grace!

OK, I'll listen to the birds while I wait. Peaceful, cheeping birds. *Cheep, cheep, cheep. Cheep, cheepity, cheepy, cheep.* Actually, birds are super **ANNOYING!** I wish they'd be quiet! Dumb birds are **stressing** me out.

Perhaps I should listen to the wind in the trees. *Rustle, rustle, rustle* . . . honestly, trees are kind of boring.

AHHH!

Maybe I should chat to someone to pass the time. But the only kids near me are Clover Williams and her annoying besties, Clem and Harper! **UGH**—they're taking **selfies** with Clover's phone. We aren't supposed to have phones at school, but of course Clover's snuck hers onto the playground. I can't believe Clover and I were ever friends.

Ugh, Otti and Sienna are laughing **again!** My sandwich is sticking in my throat.

Wait a second, I just looked at my watch and five minutes and thirty seconds have passed! Grace's presentation must be so good, my friends have **LOST TRACK OF TIME!!!**

Grace

Thursday, 1.37 p.m.,
in the library

Izzy is such an **attention-seeker!** She just came sprinting over to the Friendship Tree and **interrupted** the end of my talk.

'**It's my go!**' she yelled at our friends. They turned, but I refused to even look at Izzy.

The kindy kids nearby gaped, including one little girl who had her finger up her nose.

'You set the stopwatch wrong!' Izzy told Sienna.

Just then, the stopwatch **beeped**.

'No, I didn't,' Sienna said, clicking the button to quiet it. 'You're a minute early.'

I bet Izzy still thinks Sienna set her stopwatch wrong, even though Sienna's never wrong and she's **BETTER** at maths than Izzy.

I'd lifted my chin and said, 'I was almost finished anyway. I'll be in the library. Let me know what you decide.'

Then I came here and thought I'd write to help me calm down. But I'm so **nervous!** What if Izzy's talk *is* better than mine?

Otti folded her arms and nodded. They were as **SERIOUS** as judges on a TV talent show and it was making me nervous. I took a deep breath and launched into my speech.

'Today is a truly **magnifique** day . . .' I began in my loudest voice. I was so loud, the kindy kids in the sandpit kept staring.

Sienna took notes, and she and Otti laughed in all the right places. I was **seriously** good—better even than when I'd practiced in the garage!

At the end, the kindy kids clapped, even the nose-picking kid. I bowed.

'Right,' I said. 'What happens now?'

'We need to **confer**,' Sienna said.

'Maybe you could wait in the library with Grace?' Otti suggested.

I didn't go straight to the library. Instead, I stood in the corridor near the door, peering out at Sienna and Otti under the Friendship Tree. They were **super-serious**. They shook their heads. They frowned. I had no idea what any of it meant, but I was **DYING** to know if I'd won!

'But the competition's **tomorrow!'** Grace said. Her voice was high-pitched and breathy—she didn't sound like herself at all.

Otti did a nervous little ballet step. She **HATES** upsetting anyone. But Sienna gave her a little nudge.

'You'll have to decide for **yourselves**,' Otti said bravely.

'Thanks for **SABOTAGING** my talk,' Grace said, turning to me. 'You burst in before I was finished.'

'Hey, it's not my fault Sienna set the stopwatch wrong,' I said.

'Excuse me?' Sienna said, her eyes bugging out. 'I did not. You counted the minutes wrong!'

(NOT TRUE!)

'You sabotaged me because you were too **SCARED** to let me finish. After all, I actually did some work on my talk,' Grace said. 'I bet you spent about two minutes on yours!'

Whoa, that **STUNG!** Do you know that superhero who has lasers that burst out of his eyes to destroy bad guys? Well, I felt like that. **Hot lasers** were about to blast out of my eyes and burn Grace into **ASHES!**

I still can see Grace's face as I'm writing this—she got even **angrier** than Zeus does when she sees our neighbour's labradoodle! I keep thinking about what Grace said. What did she mean about **always** giving in to me?

Grace is the twin everyone **adores**—even Smelodie and our dumb cat love her, and they don't adore **ANYONE!**

'Grace is such a kind girl,' everyone always says; 'Grace is a real quiet achiever'; 'Grace always tries her best'. Worst of all, 'Izzy, why can't you be more like Grace?' Blah, blah, **BLAH!**

Everything's so **easy** for Grace! She gets whatever she wants without asking. Not like me. I have to **FIGHT** for everything!

Well, at least I know **how** to fight! And since both of us are still doing France at the presentations tomorrow, I know one sure-fire way to fight . . . and **WIN!**

Grace

Thursday, 8.38 p.m.

I was so **upset** about what Izzy said about my talk, that I could only pick at Dad's cabbage rolls for dinner, and he makes the **best** cabbage rolls. Dad and Mum were giving each other worried-parent looks but I ignored them. After dinner, I shut myself in our room.

I kept hearing Izzy say, 'No-one wants to watch a **boring old** tour guide go on about **boring old** museums!'

What if she was right? What if my talk was **boring?!**

I'm not like Izzy, who makes people laugh. I know she'll put in lots of **smashing** and **bashing** and **blood** and **gore** from the revolution. Even if Izzy's France talk is ridiculous, she'll do something crazy and everyone will talk about it for weeks.

Will anyone even **REMEMBER** my talk?

Zeus head-butted my legs.

'Zeus,' I said. 'I need to **beat** Izzy.'

She meowed.

'How can I make my talk **more interesting?**' I asked her.

Zeus **heaved** herself onto my bed, leaving a dent on the covers. She settled on my stripy shirt and beret, which I'd laid out, ready for tomorrow.

'Zeus!' I said. 'Get off my costume!'

But then it hit me—Zeus was giving me the answer. A **MIND-BLOWING COSTUME** would fix my talk!

Zeus is the **cleverest cat that ever lived!**

I opened our laptop and searched the internet for artistic costume ideas. On a Halloween page, I found something perfect. I read through the instructions, and yes, we had everything I'd need to make a France costume that **no-one** would ever forget.

I ran through the living room in my slippers and headed out into the dark garden. Light seeped out from under the garage door. I pushed it open.

'What are you doing in here?' Izzy said, glaring. She was wearing her French revolution costume with the beanie pulled down low.

'Since Mum and Dad paid for the house, I own the garage just as much as you,' I said airily.

I went around the garage and gathered:

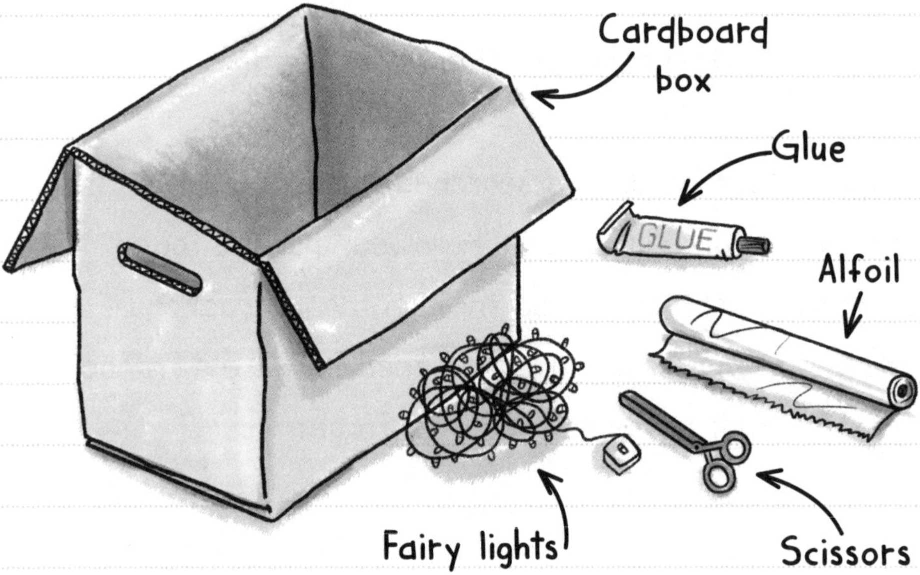

Then I **swept** out of the garage, the door slamming behind me.

Back at my desk, I set to work following the video tutorial, singing as I cut and glued.

An hour later, I was done. I put on my costume and looked at myself in the mirror. Sure, I'd cut the face-hole a bit small, but no-one would call my talk '**boring**' after seeing me in this!

I heard footsteps in the corridor.

'Elodie, can you come here, please?' I called.

Elodie poked her head around the door.

'What do you think?' I asked.

'**WOW**,' Elodie said, eyes bulging. 'Did you make that all by yourself?'

'I did,' I said proudly.

'It's, uh, **impressive**,' Elodie said. 'But aren't you giving a presentation? How are people going to hear you properly if you're wearing that?'

I shifted the costume so my mouth was at the face-hole, although I couldn't see anything.

'Like this,' I said loudly, then shifted the hole so I could see again.

'It's **big**, isn't it?' Elodie said. 'Won't you bump into things?'

'I can bend my knees and turn sideways, see?' I said, showing her.

'Yeah, I see,' she said. 'But, err, don't you think it's a little . . . **over-the-top?**'

I smiled kindly at her through the face–hole, using only my eyes. Elodie might be a maths and music **genius**, but when it comes to art and design, she knows **nothing**.

'That's the whole point,' I told her. '**MORE IS MORE**, Elodie! No–one will forget my France presentation when I'm wearing this.'

Elodie raised her eyebrows.

'That's for sure,' she said, and wandered off to her room.

I ignored her **bad vibes**. Elodie had said she was impressed, that was the main thing. *I'm* impressed. I've spent ages looking at myself in the mirror, admiring my giant Eiffel Tower costume. It's so big! So shiny!

Tomorrow, I'll knock their **chaussettes** (that's 'socks' in French) off!

Izzy

Friday morning,
in class

Finding rhyming words online is easy. But putting them into a rap that makes sense is much trickier. That's the **ART** part of being a **HIP-HOP ARTIST**.

'Revolution' and 'solution' are fine, and I can even work in 'constitution' and 'execution'. But 'pollution' is hard, and what does 'Aleutian' even mean?! After slaving in the garage all evening, I finally ended up with what I think is my **best rap yet**. I can picture how it will go down . . .

BRILLIANT, huh? (Sorry about last time, Mr Rafael. I promise if I cartwheel, I'll check where the microphone stand is.)

Grace doesn't have a **hope**, not that she knows it. She totally ignored me this morning. When we left the house for school, she hurried off like an **Olympic walker** with her bum waggling, even though she was lugging a big shopping bag. She spent last night working on whatever was in there. I spent the whole walk to school wondering what it was.

Whatever it is, she doesn't stand a **CHANCE** against the **super-rhymester**, Izzy T!

When I got inside the school gates, the playground was buzzing with students wearing **ORANGE** for Harmony Day. Orange socks, scrunchies, t-shirts and dresses flashed past as kids ran about playing tip and handball. I'd completely **forgotten** to wear orange. Oh well!

I saw Sienna striding over in an orange button-down and jeans, and we walked over to the **Friendship Tree** together, where Otti was doing stretches with an orange scarf in her hair. In the grass beside her was a paper bag.

'Finally!' Otti said. 'Where's Grace?'

'No idea,' I said, ignoring the disappointed looks on her and Sienna's faces. Obviously they were hoping we'd **made up**.

I pointed to Otti's paper bag to change the subject.

'What's that?' I asked.

'**American saltwater taffy**,' Otti said proudly, offering the bag. 'I loved it when we lived there. You were right about those cookies, by the way—Mum was really upset I'd used all her spices. But my taffy is soooooo much better!'

Sienna eyed the bag like Zeus eyes the nail-clippers when Dad's about to trim her claws.

'Have you tried them?' she asked.

'Yep, I tasted the **mix** while I was making it,' Otti said.

So Sienna and I both popped one into our mouths. A rich, creamy taste spread over my tongue. Otti's taffies were **DELICIOUS!**

I was going to ask what the difference was between 'taffy' and 'toffee', when I realised my teeth were **STUCK TOGETHER**. Otti's taffy was so strong and sticky, you could have built a brick wall with it. Sienna's eyes widened like she was drowning.

'Guys, what's wrong?' Otti asked nervously.

'Sis 'uck,' I mumbled.

Sienna was going crosseyed, flapping her hands and pointing at her mouth. Finally, she pulled a pen and piece of paper from her bag and wrote:

'Oh no!' Otti said. 'Can I help?'

But Sienna waved her away. I chewed for what felt like ten minutes—the stuff was like **SUPERGLUE** and my jaw felt like it had been lifting **weights** in the gym. Finally, when I thought I'd never open my mouth again, my teeth came **unstuck**. But Sienna kept making these sad, little moans and massaging her face.

Finally, Sienna took up the pen again and wrote:

DENTAL DISASTER!!!
GOING TO THE OFFICE! ☹

Otti was **HORRIFIED**.

'I'm so sorry, Sienna,' she said, but Sienna had already picked up her bag and hurried off.

'What am I going to do?' Otti wailed. She tossed the paper bag on the grass. 'I can't serve those! Heaps of Year 5 and 6 kids have braces. Mr Rafael will be so **upset** with me if I don't do something for my "World Around Us" project!'

'The taffy tastes delicious,' I said, trying to cheer her up. 'It's just a little **chewy**. If you're going to throw them away, can I have them?'

'Sure,' Otti said sadly. 'But if you **ruin** your teeth, don't tell your parents you got it from me.'

I stuck the paper bag into the side pocket of my backpack. If I get sick of chewing, they'll be brilliant for **pranking** an irritating teenager whose name rhymes with **BELODIE POMIC!**

Grace

Friday, 3.34 p.m.

This morning started really well. The only drawback on Harmony Day is that our outfits have to contain **orange** and I look **terrible** in orange! I'd come up with a clever solution: my apricot-pink top. It wasn't truly orange, but it was orange enough to get away with. I'd paired it with my favourite skirt because the apricot really pops against the warm floral pattern.

As soon as I got to school, I slipped into the Year 5 classroom and peeked at my Eiffel Tower. Just looking at it gave me a flutter of happiness. Instead of **très dérangé**, I was **TRÈS EXCITEE** (that means 'very excited'), because in a few hours I was going to **wow** the whole school! Carefully, I slid the bag on top of the shelves where it would be safe.

When class started, I took my seat beside Otti, who was strangely quiet the whole morning. All lessons after morning session were cancelled, so as soon as the bell rang, the **Harmony Day Activities** began!

We had the Friendship Tree to ourselves, so Otti and I ate our morning tea alone. But instead of stretching or laughing and talking like usual, Otti barely said **a word**.

'Are you OK?' I asked.

'Yep,' she said.

She clearly didn't want to talk about whatever it was that was **upsetting** her, so I watched the teachers and students set up the Harmony Day **stalls**.

Otti and I wandered from activity to activity, but she just wasn't herself. Usually, seeing our principal sitting on the ground **solemnly chanting** and tapping a little gong would send us into fits of laughter, but she didn't even **giggle**.

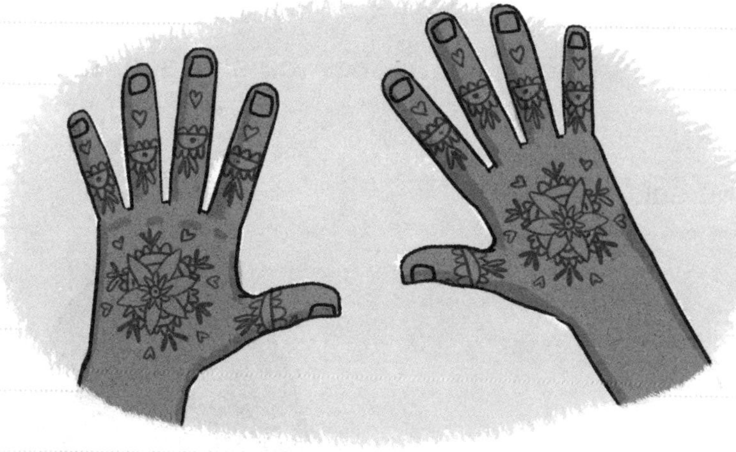

We ended up at Year 6 teacher Ms Kapoor's henna stall, where she was painting **DAINTY SWIRLS** on the back of kids' hands. She'd changed into these beautiful Indian pants and top and had a red dot on her forehead. Otti said her outfit was called a **salwar kameez** and the dot was called a **bindi**. Her mum sometimes wore them on special occasions, too.

I was dying to give **henna painting** a go, but I thought it would look strange with my Eiffel Tower costume.

'How about I paint your hands?' I said to Otti, thinking it might **cheer** her up.

Otti smiled, but underneath she was sad, sad, **sad**.

'OK,' she said.

I thought I did a **PRETTY GOOD JOB**. With Ms Kapoor's help, I covered Otti's hands with plastic wrap to protect the henna from **smudging** until it dried.

Then, we went to the toilets so I could wash my own hands.

As Otti slumped against the basin, she asked, 'Have you seen Sienna since this morning?'

'I think her parents picked her up,' I said, shaking water off my hands. I'd overheard the secretary telling Mr Rafael at the start of class. 'Something happened to her braces and she had to go to **the dentist**.'

Otti's face crumpled. 'It's all my **fault**,' she wailed.

I put my arm around Otti. In between sobs, she told me what had happened.

'It was an **accident**,' I said. 'Sienna knows you didn't mean to stick her teeth together.'

Otti's face was swollen and crumpled.

'But I mess everything up!' she said. 'I'm no good at **anything**, and now I've ruined my friend's braces because I can't even **cook!** I bet Sienna's going to miss her presentation because of me.'

I hated Otti putting herself down that way.

'You *don't* get everything wrong,' I said. 'You're AMAZING at **music** and **dance!** Maybe you should do what my Baka says and play to your strengths? That means putting **effort** into what you're good at, instead of **worrying** about what you're maybe not as good at.'

Sniffing, Otti admired her hands.

'Thanks,' she said. 'You're the best. And my hands are so PRETTY. You're so good at art and school and everything.'

'But not **dancing**,' I said, and reminded her of the PE dance routine we had to do last year. 'Remember how I accidentally smacked Sienna in the face and she had that bruise on her cheek for weeks?'

'I remember,' Otti said, smiling through her tears.

'That was **hard** for me, but it was **easy** for you,' I said.

Otti stared at me. Her feet tapped a little **pattern** on the concrete.

'What?' I said, touching my cheek. 'Have I got henna on my face?'

'No,' she said. 'I think . . .'

But I never found out what Otti thought, because the bell sounded and **the principal's** voice droned over the loudspeaker.

'The HARMONY DAY COMPETITION will begin at 2 p.m. Any student who is presenting should get their costume on and report to the hall to register. Competitors will then have **an hour** to rehearse.'

'That's me,' I said to Otti.

'Good luck,' she said, and hugged me. I was glad to see she looked more **cheerful** again.

I hurried off to my classroom, lifted down my bag and carefully slipped on my Eiffel Tower costume. I was ready! I shuffled into the corridor, bumping into the door frame—**oops**. Halfway down the corridor, I heard singing coming from another classroom and peered in.

Through the face-hole of my costume, I saw Clover Williams singing in a gentle, throaty language as her friends clapped their hands and drummed the table in time. They sounded like **REAL PERFORMERS** that people **paid** to see. Even in my Eiffel Tower, I couldn't compete with that!

As I stepped away, the corner of my costume knocked the door and it **creaked**. I froze, hoping desperately that Clover hadn't heard.

Inside the classroom, the singing stopped. **Nooooo!**

I was **shuffling** as fast as I could down the corridor when the classroom door opened behind me.

'Grace Tomic? Is that you?!'

I winced, and slowly turned to face the voice.

'Grace, it *is* you! What *are* you wearing?' Clover said in a fake sweet voice.

She knew my costume was meant to be the Eiffel Tower. I was glad she could only see my eyes, because my cheeks were **burning**.

'I know! You're doing Japan, since you're dressed as a **giant robot**,' Clover went on.

Honestly, I wanted to **disappear!** Was my costume truly that bad? Was it **HORRIBLY EMBARRASSING** and I'd been fooling myself?

'It's the Eiffel Tower,' I said, keeping my voice steady. 'See the shape?'

'Oh!' Clover said, pretending to be surprised. She tilted her head and **squinted**. 'What do you guys think?'

Clem and Harper tilted their heads too and **shrugged**.

'Nope,' Clover said, shaking her wig. 'Still looks like a giant robot to me.'

I swallowed my tears, wishing Zeus was around to bite her ankle. Clover Williams is **the worst!**

Izzy

Friday, after school

It's been a **CRAZY** day!

I was **super pumped** when Crome Dome came over the loudspeaker this afternoon. It was time to get ready for the Harmony Day presentation competition! Clutching my costume, I turned the corner to the hall and **stopped dead**.

I slumped against the lockers. Smelodie the Evil One was right. France *wasn't* original. **DOZENS** of kids were doing France!

Immediately, I thought of Grace. She'd worked **super hard** on her talk and was probably rehearsing it somewhere. I had to let her know.

I couldn't see her outside the hall. Year 6 teacher, Ms Kapoor, stood by the door, marking off names for the competition.

'Are you still doing a **presentation**, Izzy?' she asked as I drew near.

'Yep,' I said, and as Ms Kapoor marked me off, I added, 'Has Grace had her name marked off yet?'

Ms Kapoor checked her list and shook her head.

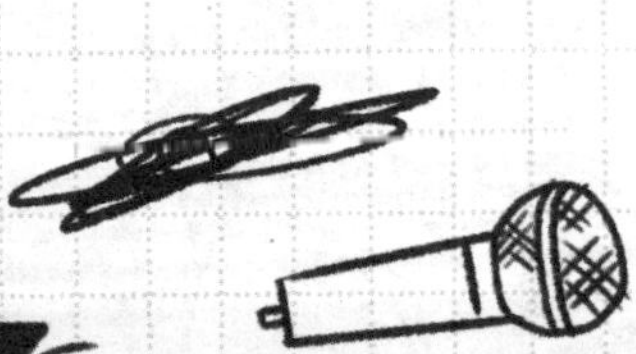

I searched under the Friendship Tree, behind the sports shed and in the library, all the places Grace would usually go to practice, but she wasn't in any of them.

Then I tried the building where the Year 5 and 6 classrooms were, and guess what I saw? At the end of the corridor, with her hands on her hips, was Clover Williams in a **flashy** costume. Her dopey friends were beside her. My gaze lasered in on Clover's schoolbag, which was just inside the classroom behind her, where **MY SQUISHY HAMBURGER KEYRING HUNG!**

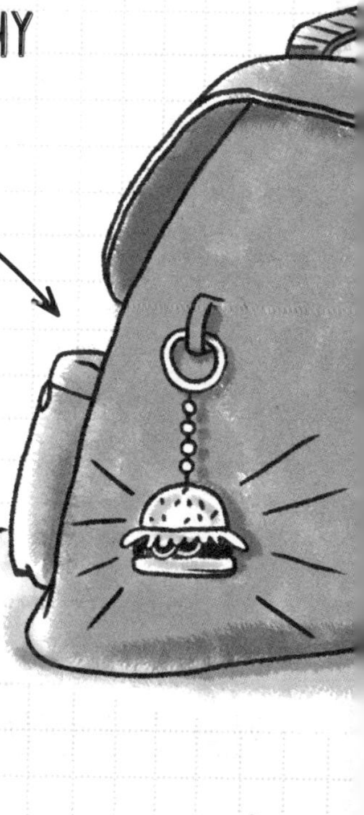

My hands curled into fists.

After a few seconds of **glaring** at my keyring, and getting sweaty and angry all over again, I realised Clover and her friends were sniggering at someone. Someone wearing . . . **a big silver box?**

'Nope. Still looks like a **giant robot** to me,' I heard Clover say.

'**Totally!**' Clem and Harper said.

'It's the Eiffel Tower and you know it,' a familiar voice replied.

It was Grace! And she sounded close to tears. My sister was **close to tears** because of Clover Williams! The superhero, hot-laser feeling throbbed behind my eyes again, except this time I was going to **BLAST CLOVER WILLIAMS INTO ASHES!**

I marched down the corridor and stood between Clover and my sister.

'At least a robot's cool,' I said to Clover. 'You're wearing so much make-up, you look like you're entering a **TODDLER BEAUTY PAGEANT**.'

'Like you know anything about **beauty**,' Clover said. 'Do you even own a hairbrush?'

'You're just scared to go up against **THE TOMIC TWINS**,' I snapped back.

Clover rolled her eyes. 'Scared to go up against a robot and whatever **lame rap** you came up with last night?'

WHOA! Had Grace overheard me practicing last night and told them about my France rap?

'As if,' I said, trying to stay cool. 'Why do you think I'd do a rap?'

'Because you did that lame rap about the houses of government where you tried to slide across the stage and **fell off the edge**,' Clem chimed in.

'And what about that science rap where you rhymed "**comet**" with "**VOMIT**"?' Harper added, and they all sniggered.

'And don't forget the Antarctica rap, where you—' Clover started.

Oh no. My Antarctica rap was coming back in horrible flashes!

But as I led her along the corridor, a corner of her Eiffel Tower knocked a schoolbag hanging from a hook, and Grace **toppled over** sideways.

'**OWWWW!**' she said, trying to stand up, but she couldn't. Not in that costume.

Clover's **hoots** and **whoops** followed us down the corridor.

In the art room, I helped Grace take off her Eiffel Tower. Underneath, she was flushed and her hair was fuzzed up.

I stared into the eyes that matched mine and we started twinning. I wasn't Izzy anymore—*we* were **ZIZANGEE**. And we felt all the **bad stuff**: hurt, guilty, sorry and embarrassed.

At the same time, we both said:

'Mee ji, Ziz.'

'Mee ji, Gee.'

That means 'I'm sorry' in our twin language.

'Sorry I said being a tour guide was a boring idea,' I said. 'It isn't. I was just **jealous**.'

'Sorry I said you copied your talk from Wikipedia,' Grace replied. She gave me a small smile. 'That was **mean**. I know you worked really hard.'

'Sorry I got us kicked out of the library,' I said.

'Actually, that was my fault,' Grace said. 'I yelled.'

'Sorry we might be Clover's **servants** all year,' I said quickly. Since we were doing apologies, it seemed a good time to get my **WORST CRIME** over with.

Grace made a face. 'Yeah, that **wasn't great**,' she said. 'We're going to have to carry her backpack, and buy her gummies, and do her homework all year.'

'She'll probably use us as footstools at lunchtime,' I said gloomily. 'Blame the **TOMIC PRIDE**.'

When I'd thrown down the bet with Clover, I'd felt **bold** and **daring** like a French revolutionary. Now I felt about as sharp as a **jumbo crayon**.

Sadly, Grace considered her Eiffel Tower costume.

'Clover's right. It does look like a **GIANT ROBOT**,' she said. 'I can't believe I was going to go onstage wearing a cardboard box covered in foil. And last night I thought it was so good!'

'It is good,' I said. 'And it's definitely the Eiffel Tower. Anyway, forget that stuff—' I didn't want to get onto the topic of raps, because Grace would see my face and **KNOW** I'd come up with a France one. '—we've got a bigger problem. **Everyone's** doing France!'

As I told her what I'd seen, Grace pressed her lips together.

'So that's it,' she said. 'Neither of us can win doing France.'

'Yep,' I said. 'And if Clover wins, she's going to get Crome Dome's $100 prize *plus* she'll have us picking up her rubbish, painting her fingernails and massaging her feet for the rest of the year. If we win, we get . . .' I paused dramatically.

'. . . ONE SQUISHY HAMBURGER KEYRING.'

At that, we began to giggle. Not only had we been fighting over nothing, but I'd made the **dumbest deal ever**. It was sooooo terrible, it was funny. We couldn't stop laughing.

Grace

Friday, 8.10 p.m.

My favourite group of artists are the **Impressionists**, who did these lush paintings in purples and greens and blues. Up close, the canvases look like they've been **splattered** by kindy kids. It's only when you step back that you can see the pictures in them: the pond of water lilies, or the sun rising over the ocean.

The Harmony Day competition was kind of like an Impressionist painting I'd been standing too close to. All I could see were **messy splodges**. One splodge was the oil-paint set I wanted. Another splodge was France. The biggest splodge was Izzy blocking me from winning.

After Izzy saved me from Clover and her gang, I stepped back and saw the whole picture. This was about **Harmony Day** and the whole point of Harmony Day is . . . well, **HARMONY**.

So Izzy and I paced the art room, trying to come up with a new idea for our presentation. We were about to end up as Clover Williams's servants. I know I should have been **furious** with Izzy, but I was just glad we were speaking again. I'd really **missed** her.

Then the loudspeaker hummed and Mr Crome's voice filled the art room.

'We've had a late addition to the Harmony Day activities,' he droned. 'Rocky Point Primary is getting a **surprise dance lesson** before the competition. All students please go to the playground. Repeat, all students to the playground.'

Izzy and I shared a look, then hurried out to join the throng.

'What's going on?' asked a girl wearing a striped shirt and beret.

'**No idea**,' a boy said, holding a tricorn hat. 'But I really need to practice my speech!'

Mr Crome stood on the basketball court with the microphone. The portable speaker was beside him.

'RPP, we have a **treat** this afternoon,' Mr Crome said. He looked relaxed for once, so maybe the meditation had done him good. 'I'd like to welcome Otti Ogawa, who's going to lead us in a surprise dance session for Harmony Day.'

Izzy and I **shrieked**!

Mr Crome passed Otti the microphone and it **screeched** with feedback. Kids groaned and covered their ears.

'Um, hi,' Otti said timidly, holding the microphone like it was a dangerous snake. 'I'm going to show you some **Bhangra** steps for beginners. **Bhangra** is a style of dance that comes from the northern part of **India**, where my mother was born, and it was created by farmers over five hundred years ago. I hope you like it.'

Shyly, Otti passed the microphone back, and twangy, bouncy music blasted through the speakers.

Dhamaal

Put your arms in the air and hop from foot to foot, lifting the knees.

Bedi

Do a bouncing step-touch.

Punjab

Bounce from side to side, tapping each foot across your body.

I'm here to tell you that even if you're a hopeless dancer like me, Bhangra is so much **FUN!**

Between the kids bouncing around like **kangaroos**, I saw a familiar figure striding towards us.

'Sienna!' I called, dodging around dancing kids to meet her.

'My face is still **numb**,' she yelled, prodding her cheek. 'But the orthodontist said I can do my talk!'

Izzy raced over and the three of us **danced** Bhangra at the back of the crowd. As the music got faster and everyone bounced harder, Izzy shot me a look.

Want to? her face said.

Sure! I silently replied.

Izzy and I grabbed hands and started to **spin**. Faster and faster we spun, until the playground blurred and Rocky Point Primary disappeared and we were just **ZIZANGEE, TOGETHER FOREVER**.

Then our hands slipped apart and we wobbled away. Giggling, I landed in the sandpit and Izzy ended up under the Friendship Tree.

As I sat up, an image flashed in front of me: Dad's photo of Baka and Great-Aunt Vesna as girls, **spinning** just like Izzy and me. Baka had told us stories about growing up as twins when their country was part of a bigger country called **Yugoslavia**, and I thought how strange it was that countries could disappear and new ones appear, simply because someone decided it. Yugoslavia didn't exist anymore . . . **oh!**

I leapt up, brushing sand from my hair. I'd had the **BEST AND CRAZIEST IDEA EVER!**

Izzy

Friday night, late

It's late, but I *have* to finish writing about what went down this afternoon before I forget! (I'm buzzing again as I write this. Grace's right—a diary *is* a bit like a friend who listens. And never talks back, **HAAAAA!** It's a pretty good way to sort out my thoughts.)

As we ran into the hall for the competition this afternoon, Grace and I were **BUZZING**.

Sienna was already on stage talking about **Scotland**. It wasn't going well. Kids were fidgeting and yawning, and one boy was asleep.

We snuck up the side aisle and slipped backstage. Ms Kapoor was there with her clipboard to **direct** the competitors when it was their turn. Her eyebrows shot up.

'Where have you girls been?!' she whispered.

'Working on our talk,' I replied softly.

'Rehearsal time ended forty minutes ago,' she said, then sighed. 'Well, you're here now. Who's first?'

'We're **together**,' we said, and Ms Kapoor marked that on her list.

As Sienna clicked to her next slide, Crome Dome stepped on stage.

'Unfortunately, we'll have to **end** it there,' he said, taking the microphone. 'RPP, please put your hands together for Sienna Burns and her complete history of Scotland!'

Scattered claps sounded across the hall. Sienna walked off stage in a **HUFF**.

'*Complete history?*' she whispered, glowering at Crome Dome. 'I didn't even get to the Vikings!'

On stage, Crome Dome checked the piece of paper in his hand.

'Next up are the **CCCs** with their presentation about Ireland.'

Clapping and soulful singing floated out from the other side of the stage. We peered over to see Clover singing as she walked onstage, followed by Clem and Harper clapping and singing in harmony. In perfect time, the trio started to **Irish dance**. Their arms were straight by their sides and their tapping feet provided the tricky rhythm.

I hate to admit it, but the CCCs were **TERRIFIC** at singing and Irish dancing. Then, a heavy beat cut in over the sound system and **pop music** blasted through the hall! Clover did a body roll to the new music, and Clem and Harper repeated the move.

I recognised the routine from seeing them practice it in the playground—they'd learnt it at their dance school. Everyone in the hall went crazy, and even the snoozing boy woke up. Kids were **clapping and whistling** as the music pounded and Clover, Clem and Harper tore up the stage. Irish or not, the CCCs' performance was unfortunately awesome, ending with **power poses.**

How could Grace and I beat *THAT*? We were about to become Clover's slaves for a whole year!

I turned to Grace. *We've got no chance,* I said with my face.

Her eyes shining, Grace stuck out her fist.

See, even though my sister seems dreamy and gentle, she's also tougher than me. She was saying, *We can do this!*

I made a fist and bumped hers.

'**Stronger together,**' we whispered at the same time.

I felt like I'd taken a swig of a tangy energy drink.

As Clover, Clem and Harper sashayed down the steps to everyone clapping like crazy, I headed for the back of the hall.

'Oh, you're too sweet,' I heard Clover saying to the younger girls clustering around her in the aisle. 'We go to Broadway School of Dance, but it's **very exclusive** and only **THE BEST** dancers get in. Honestly, I wouldn't bother to audition.

You haven't got a chance.'

When Clover and her friends had taken their seats, and the applause finally died down, Crome Dome took the microphone again.

'And for our final Harmony Day presentation, I'd like to welcome the **TOMIC TWINS**,' he said, and walked off.

Grace stepped on stage wearing a school dress we'd taken from the lost property box. Her footsteps echoed as she walked to the microphone clutching her palm cards. Her face was pale and her left knee was shaking.

'Come on, Gee,' I whispered, trying to beam my thoughts to her. '**You've got this!**'

I tapped the screen of the tablet we'd borrowed from our classroom.

'When people think of Europe, they think of France, or Italy or Germany,' Grace said in a small voice. 'But I want to tell you about the unusual country my family comes from. **Bosnia and Herzegovina** is in southern Europe, and it's where our Baka—that means "grandmother"—was born.

'Bosnia and Herzegovina has a long name, but a short history. In fact, the country was only created in **1992**. When Baka was my age, her town was part of a bigger country called Yugoslavia, where lots of different groups of people lived,' Grace continued, her voice growing more confident. Baka is a **CROAT**, which is the name of one of the ethnic groups there. This part of Europe has a **bloody history**, with wars breaking out and the borders of countries changing depending on who won those wars.' Grace walked to the side of the stage. 'Like me and my sister . . .' she said, and disappeared off stage.

Everyone gazed around, **confused**.

'Huh?' someone said.

'Where did she go?' someone else hissed.

'. . . like me and my sister, Baka is an **IDENTICAL TWIN**,'
I said, from the back of the hall.

Hundreds of heads swivelled to see me, dressed identically to Grace in a lost-property dress. **Gasps and murmurs** rose from the audience. Someone laughed.

'How did she get there?' a kindy kid asked.

As a teacher shushed him, I glanced down at the tablet.

'Baka and her sister, Great-Aunt Vesna, were as **close** as anything,' I went on, walking down the aisle towards the stage. 'They shared a bedroom in an apartment in the city.'

I tapped the tablet and a picture of Yugoslavian **apartment blocks** from the 1960s appeared.

'Baka and Vesna did everything together. They were best friends as well as sisters. When they were eighteen, they heard about **special visas** to Australia. Getting a visa meant they could move here to **work**. But their family didn't have enough money to send both girls, so they decided only Baka would go. Vesna would stay in Yugoslavia and follow later.'

I climbed the steps onto the stage.

'For the first time ever, the twins said **goodbye**,' I said loudly. 'But . . .'

I stepped backstage as Grace stood up in the middle of the audience. The kids near her **gasped and giggled**.

With everyone's gaze on Grace, I slipped out the exit and headed to my next position.

'. . . But, Baka and Vesna didn't know just how **long** that goodbye would be for,' Grace said loudly. She was working her way out of the row to the aisle. 'Baka married a man with a Croatian background, my grandfather, and started a **NEW LIFE** here in our country. Great-Aunt Vesna stayed in Yugoslavia.'

As Grace walked to the back of the hall, everyone turned to watch her.

'All that time, the sisters wrote **letters**, and talked on the **phone** and sometimes took **trips** to visit each other,' she went on, opening the back exit. 'This was before texting, and video calls and chat groups. But then . . .'

Grace ducked out the door.

'. . . But then . . .' I said, **popping out** of the girl's toilets across the other side of the hall.

The audience laughed. I waited until the laughter died away, then clicked the tablet.

'. . . a string of **terrible** wars broke out,' I finished.

Everyone went quiet, staring at the image that had appeared on the screen: a scene of a bombed-out city.

'Baka watched from Australia as the country she grew up in **DISAPPEARED**,' I said, walking towards the stage. 'Every day, Baka saw footage of her hometown being destroyed. She didn't know if her sister was alive or dead. For months, she waited . . . until one day, she got a phone call. Great-Aunt Vesna had **survived** the bombings, living in a basement for months without heating, or proper food or even sunlight. The twins cried and laughed on that phone call. And their **bond stayed strong**.'

I tapped the tablet, and Dad's old photo of Baka and Great-Aunt Vesna as girls, dancing together, appeared on the screen.

Yugoslavia broke into a group of new countries, including Croatia, Slovenia and Serbia. The area that my Baka had lived in, and where my Great-Aunt Vesna still lives, is called Bosnia and Herzegovina—**a new country with two parts to it,** one in the north and one in the south. The country isn't very rich. It still has many problems. It's made up of different groups who struggle to live together in peace. But both regions are part of the whole.'

I walked on stage and smiled at Grace in the wings, who joined me and took my hand. Together, we stood in front of the picture of our relatives.

'**A bit like us**,' we finished together.

As we walked off holding hands, the crowd broke into cheers and applause. I was **tingling!** Suddenly, I wished Baka was here. She would have **LOVED** it!

Because we were last, Grace and I waited backstage while the teachers acting as judges talked for **ages** across the other side of the stage.

I know it sounds corny, but for a little while, I didn't care about winning. All that mattered was that I had my sister back.

I'm not an angel, though. After a few seconds, that feeling faded and I was **DESPERATE** to beat Clover Williams again!

The judges whispered. They frowned. They nodded. Finally, Crome Dome walked on stage and took the microphone.

'We've had some inspirational presentations today at RPP, and it's been tough to choose a winner. In the end, though, the judges agreed. The **$100 voucher prize** goes to Grace and Isabel Tomic. Not only did they tell us a family story about **RESILIENCE**, but we were introduced to a country we knew very little about.'

WHOA! We'd WON! The Tomic twins had WON!!

As we walked on stage into the lights, I spotted Sienna and Otti clapping madly. Mr Crome shook our hands and handed us an envelope, then school was dismissed.

As the hall emptied, Otti and Sienna ran over to us.

'**CONGRATULATIONS!**' Otti said, doing a little spin.

'That was **fascinating**,' Sienna said. 'Why haven't you told us that before?'

Grace and I looked at each and shrugged. In a **happy daze**, we went to get our bags, with kids congratulating us all the way.

In front of our classroom, we heard a familiar voice.

'Worst Harmony Day ever!' Clover said loudly.

Clover and her crew were **PRETENDING** they hadn't seen us. Yeah, sure.

'Sienna's talk was so boring, everyone fell asleep,' Clem said.

Sienna gave us an awkward smile, then stared at her feet.

'And what kind of dance was Otti teaching? It was completely weird,' Harper said.

Otti looked crushed.

'And as for the twins,' Clover went on, 'they're completely **talentless**. They didn't dance, or sing or anything—they just talked. **DULLSVILLE!**'

That girl is **LETHAL!** I couldn't take any more.

'Otti doesn't even need a routine,' I said loudly, stepping into the room and facing Clover. 'She's a brilliant dancer. And Sienna knows more about history than you ever will. Anyway, aren't you forgetting something?' I pointed to Clover's backpack.

With a **sulky pout**, Clover unclipped the keyring.

'Have the dumb thing, if you want it so much!' she said, tossing my squishy hamburger keyring under the storage cupboard.

'Gee, thanks,' I said, rolling my eyes.

While Clover and her crew sniggered, I crouched and felt around under the cupboard, ignoring other squishy but disgusting things (**UGHHH!**), until I found it.

'**Aha!**' I stood up and displayed my keyring.

'Anyway, you're welcome to it,' Clover said, fishing around in her backpack. 'Because look what we found lying around.' She waved the paper bag with **OTTI'S SALTWATER TAFFY** in it.

Clover must have taken it from my backpack. Yet *more* **proof** that Clover *was* a thief, and the one who'd **stolen** my squishy hamburger keyring!

Otti stuck out her bottom lip. Sienna's eyes bugged out. Neither said a word.

Grace flashed me a look. *Should we say something?*, her look said. *After all, Clover has braces.*

I raised my eyebrows a fraction, replying, *NO WAY!*

'I just love taffy,' Clover said, smugly. '**Yum, yum!**'

We watched in silence as Harper and Clem fished out a piece each, then Clover grabbed **TWO** and shoved them into her mouth. She chewed. A blissed-out look spread over her face.

Clover turned to Clem and Harper, and said: 'Mmmm-hmm . . . **HMMMM?!**' Her face changed. She **grunted** and **stamped** her foot, trying to open her mouth. She was so **ANGRY**, her wig looked like it was going to burst into flumes!

'Sorry, Clover,' Grace said sweetly. 'We can't understand what you're saying.'

'Talk later,' I added. 'If you're lucky!'

The four of us fast-walked out to the playground and collapsed in a **fit of giggles** under the Friendship Tree.

Grace

Sunday, 7.55 p.m.

Friday night after we'd won the competition, Izzy and I lay in our beds. Moonlight filtered in through the open window, and Zeus was **snuggled** between my head and the wall, grooming my hair with her tongue.

'We beat Clover, didn't we, good girl?' I said to her, as she licked my hair.

Zeus gave a happy **chirp**. I swear she's almost human!

'I can't believe you let her do that,' Izzy said, making a **gagging** sound. 'It's disgusting.'

Izzy doesn't understand cats and never will, so I've given up explaining.

'What shall we do with the money?' I said instead.

We talked about **splitting** the prize and putting it towards my paint set and Izzy's boots, but decided not to. We would save up our pocket money for those. We decided there was something **MORE IMPORTANT** we needed to spend our prize money on.

When we'd agreed on our plan and switched out the light, an awkward silence fell. The silence had a question in it. It had been a few days. Were we getting **too old** for our twin goodnight?

Then, '**Eepug, Gee**.' Izzy's voice came through the darkness.

'**Eepug, Ziz**,' I replied.

And Zeus started to purr, because cats know everything.

Yesterday, we spoke to Mum about our plan. And this afternoon, Mum drove Otti, Sienna and us to the Rock & Spring Trampoline Park. The four of us had been talking about going **forever**, but it had always been a bit expensive.

At the counter, Izzy and I handed over our $100 voucher. It cost $20 each to bounce for as long as we wanted, so we had enough money left for iceblocks later.

Otti did Bhangra dancing, flying between trampolines to the music. She was so **graceful**, the other jumpers stopped to watch and a few even clapped.

Izzy went to the trampoline where the teenagers were, and did **flips** and **backdrops** into the foam pit. She's so brave!

Sienna and I hung out on the smaller trampolines, having a blast **BOUNCING IT UP**.

When we stopped, sweaty and giggly, Izzy led us over to the kiosk.

'Four **iceblocks**, please,' I said, proudly pulling out our $20 voucher credit.

Sienna chose a Lemon Tang, and Otti and Izzy asked for Berry Blasts.

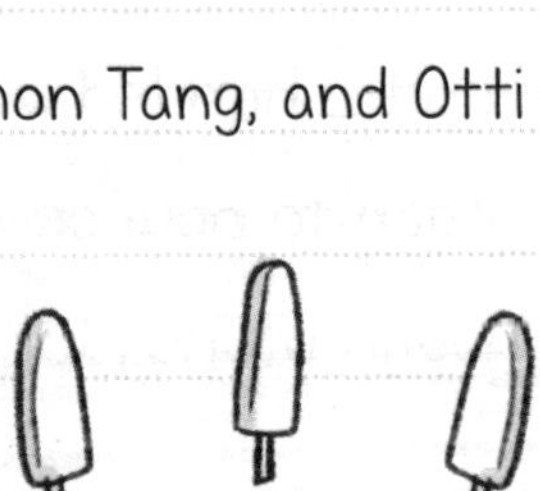

'That's the **last** Berry Blast,' the girl behind the counter said, passing Izzy her iceblock.

'But I wanted a **Berry Blast!**' I said.

Otti and Sienna stopped smiling and looked between Izzy and me as if a **volcano were about to explode**.

Then, I smiled. '**Joking**, guys. I like Lemon Tangs too, remember?' I said, and Otti wilted with relief.

Stay tuned for more

THE TOP SECRET DIARIES OF TWIN SISTERS

TWINNING

in

SKIPPING STARS.

Coming soon.